Survivor

Richard Charlemagne

ISBN: 979-8-6434-32944

CONTENTS

ACKNOWLEDGMENTS

At the point of finishing this paper, I'd like to express my sincere thanks to all those who have lent me hands. I'd like to take this opportunity to show my sincere gratitude to my readers. Many thanks for your attention and encouragement and support!

1 CHAPTER PSYCHOLOGIST

"Himani," a schoolgirl said. "Here's somebody for you."

"What's her name?" asked Himani.

"I don't know," Himani's classmate said. "He said he is your brother."

"I am the only child in the family," Himani stared at her classmate in disbelief.

"Where is he?" asked Himani.

"Over there," the schoolgirl answered.

"Thank you," said Himani.

Himani climbed the rickety wooden stairway. She paused at the top of the stairs, doubtful as to which way to go next.

"Where are you?" she asked.

The corridor would ordinarily have been full of people. There was no one.

"Where are you?" her voice echoed in the big empty corridor.

Suddenly, the window blew open in the strong gale. She opened a door and a cat whipped in. A figure loomed out of the mist.

"Who are you?" she asked.

The figure didn't answer, and shortly afterwards he left. She followed him up the steps into the top of the building. Strange to say, the figure went out of sight suddenly.

"Where are you?" she asked.

It was a bit chilly and empty hereabouts. Suddenly, someone gave her a push, and she missed her footing and fell headlong down the roof of the building...

When she woke up, she saw a doctor.

"Are you feeling better?" the doctor asked.

"Nightmares kept me awake all night," she answered.

"It's time for your tablets," the doctor said to her.

She took down the tablets in one gulp. Himani soon quieted down and fell asleep. She woke up to the sound of sirens, "what's the matter?"

"The building is on fire," a nurse said.

"What should I do?" she asked.

"Follow me," the nurse answered.

She hopped out of bed quickly. Instantly people fled from the building in disorder.

"Don't panic," a doctor talked loudly, but no one paid him any attention.

Himani was crushed out of the crowd. The air was thick with acrid smoke from the fires. The smoke almost choked her. She crawled on all fours to a nearby room and paused to catch her breath. Himani stood aghast at the terrible sight. A young man lay weltering in blood.

"What's the matter with you?" she asked.

Himani found a pistol and bent down, picked up it. Suddenly the door burst open and firemen rushed in...

She awoke from a vivid dream with her hands pressed over her face. Himani always woke up from the dream about the murder case without any idea why those appeared in the dream. There was an impressive array of pill bottles stacked on the desk. Out of sheer boredom she picked up a pill bottle, "hypnotic."

Her mind dwelt on what had passed. Just then, the door opened and her father came in.

"How do you feel?" her father asked.

She gave an honest account of what transpired.

"Give me the pill bottle," having heard this, her father became angry.

Her father went directly to the doctor's office and knocked on the door.

"Come in, please." a doctor said.

"What is it used for?" her father put the pill bottle on the table.

Her father couldn't help noticing that the doctor colored slightly.

"She is in need of a rest," the doctor said.

"Are you sure this medicine will cure my daughter?" her father looked at him.

"You mean the nightmare!" the doctor asked.

Her father nodded his head.

"Your daughter is recovering from a heart transplant operation," the doctor said.

"How much money do you truly need?" her father asked.

"What do you mean?" the doctor asked.

"Is this money enough for your greed?" her father opened an envelope and fanned out a stack of new five hundred rupees bills.

"Listen, the operation was very successful. You and I both know every drug has side effects." the doctor said.

"In other words, you are powerless to this disease." her father asked.

"Your daughter needs a psychologist," the doctor said.

"What did you say?" her father grabbed him by the collar.

Honestly, her father didn't fully understand psychology.

"What do you want to do?" the doctor asked.

"My daughter doesn't have any psychological problems." her father said.

"Dad," his daughter asked. "Where have you been?"

"Let's go!" her father said.

"Where are we going?" she asked.

"Go home," her father answered.

"Why?"

"They describe themselves as doctors, but I feel they are quacks." her father said.

Her father was in a fury to get her out of the hospital. It was dark by the time she got home. Her illness blocked her study. She went back to studying.

"The doctor said you must have three more weeks of rest," her father said to her.

"Father," she smiled and said. "Do you believe him?"

Her father was at a loss when she asked him such a question. His wife's untimely death had a catastrophic effect on him. He devoted all his love to his daughter. From then on, he and his daughter had depended on each other for survival. Some warmhearted women acted as go-betweens for him and introduced him to some girls, but he refused. He was tender of hurting of his daughter's feeling. Her indulgent father was willing to let her do anything she wanted. She was spoilt by her father. He might be burdened by guilt and regret.

"You are going to have your dinner, get washed, and go to bed." he said.

"Yes sir, I'll get right on it." his daughter stood to attention and saluted.

He returned to his room. He was so tired that he fell asleep as soon as he went to bed. Suddenly he felt a tug at his underlinen.

"How old are you? Go back to your own room." he said.

"Dad," his daughter said, "I'm scared of the dark."

"Just this once," he said.

"Thank you, Dad." she said.

Soon she snuggled down in his arm and fell asleep. After a while, a cold gust flapped the blanket off her. She glanced across at her sleeping father. She closed the window and went back to bed. Suddenly her ears caught a faint cry. The girl looked up and saw that the voice came from a bird, which was hanging in a cage on the wall.

"Hi," she said, "what's wrong with you?"

She felt the muzzle against her back. She woke suddenly with a start.

"What's wrong with you?" her father asked.

"I'm fine," a faint smile crossed her face and faded quickly.

"Dad," she said, "it is time for you to go to work."

"Get your minds out of the color," her father said.

"What would you like to eat?" her father asked.

"Anything'll do me," she answered.

The food was on the table in seconds. Just then the phone rang.

"I'll have to go now," her father said.

Now she had grown accustomed to his sudden coming and goings. Vapidness came upon her as she stood in the empty house. Suddenly she thought out a good idea, "I must write down these occurrences."

She was so buried in her work that the noise outside the window just washed over her. Suddenly the door opened and her father came in.

"What are you writing?" her father asked.

"I write nothing," she answered.

"Why are you back so early today?" she asked.

"I asked for a day off," he said.

"I have to go and cook the dinner," he added.

"What time is it now?" his daughter asked.

"11:30," he said.

"How time flies," she said.

Her stomach bulged after the dinner. A moment later, she noticed that her diary had disappeared.

"Dad," she said, "do you see my diary?"

"I threw it in a trash can," her father said.

"Why?" she asked.

"The doctor told you to take a complete rest," he said.

"This time you're gone too far," she complained angrily.

Eventually she turned around and went back to her own room. Nightmares kept her awake all night. She dosed herself with medication. Some sedatives produced the paradoxical effect of making her more anxious. Unbeknownst to her father, she went to the hospital and she found the doctor. The doctor suggested she should find a psychiatrist. She could see her father had needled him, which might be unwise. She finally came back empty-hand. She tossed and tumbled in bed, sleeplessly. Himani pulled herself upright on the bed. When she thought about the nightmares, they all came back. These nightmares had a startling likeness to one another. The question took her by surprise and she was bewitched, bothered and bewildered. She sat on the bed thumbing through a magazine...

All at once there was someone knocking on the door.

"Come in, please."

She went to the room which the advertisement had called the psychological clinic.

"Are you the psychologist?" she asked.

I nodded my head, "perhaps you are my last customer."

"Why?"

"My mother calls me mountebank," I said.

She couldn't withhold her laughter.

I felt for my glasses and found it gone. Sweat beaded up on my forehead.

"What's wrong?" she asked.

"Do you see my glasses?" I asked.

"It's on your desk," she said.

"Thank you," I put on my glasses and eyed her up and down.

"What's the matter?" she asked.

"Are you a student?" I asked.

"I charge customer on an hourly basis," I explained.

"Don't worry. I won't be unfair to you." she said.

"I will make a partial payment in advance," she added.

"Could you interpret dreams?" she asked.

"Fortuneteller is next door," I answered.

"You misunderstand me," she said.

I owed three months back rent.

"What did you dream about?" I asked.

She gave a detailed account of what she had dreamed. My methods were not dissimilar to those used by Freud. I had to admit that I was, in fact, in difficulties.

"I shut out the dream which was too painful to dwell on," she said.

"Okay," I said, "let's call it a day."

She pulled herself upright on the bed. I began to organize materials.

"Don't tell others," she said to me.

"Don't worry about it. A psychologist who gives away confidential information about customers is not behaving professionally."

She took a book from my shelf, "have you read this book?"

I was still looking down at the materials. "That's my college textbook."

"Really?" she opened the heavy Ramayana.

"Sorry," I raised my head and said. "Do you like it?"

She nodded her head.

"Take it home," I said.

"Thank you," a smile appeared on her face.

After seeing her off, I felt a void in my heart. I spent days on end in this studio. She didn't come at all. It was silly of me to keep on waiting for her. I just cannot afford to keep myself. Just then, the phone shrilled, making me jump.

"Hello," I picked up the phone.

The other end of the telephone was a middle-aged man.

"This is Himani's father," the middle-aged man said.

"I don't know how I can possibly thank you enough," he said.

"I've got something very important to tell you," I cut in.

"I can't cure your daughter's disease," I said.

"I have complete confidence in you," he hung up the phone.

I tossed and tumbled in bed that night, sleeplessly. When I was about to fall asleep, there was a light knock on the door.

"Come in, please!" I said.

"You are looking very haggard and worn," she said.

"I had a sleepless night last night," I said.

"I am totally unsuited to the job," I added.

She stared at me, thunderstruck.

"I can't cure your disease," I said.

"But-" she was about to speak.

"Sorry," I said. "There is not much I can do it."

"I see," she heaved a deep sigh and turned and left.

After a while, there was a knock again.

"What's up?" I opened the door.

"Excuse my neglect in returning your book," she said.

"You like this book," I said. "Keep it. You can have it."

"Thank you," she smiled and said.

"You're welcome," I answered.

"What do you intend to do?" she asked.

"I don't know," I thought for a while and said.

"Could you tell me your cell-phone number?" suddenly she asked.

I turned around and wrote my cell-phone number on a paper.

"Thank you," she took the paper from my hand.

When searching for a job I favoured networking and letters on spec.

"What time is it now?" I stretched and rubbed my eyes.

The clock was striking twelve. I searched the recruitment websites thoroughly, but found nothing. I was about to go to bed when my cell-phone rang. I answered my phone and heard the familiar voice on the other end of the line.

"Hi," she said.

"What's wrong?" I asked.

"I had a nightmare," she said.

"I'm not a psychologist now."

She tried to talk to me, but I hung up on her. When I woke again, I saw 2 missed calls. She was on my blacklist. I lost hope even before I started hunting for a job. I had sent my resumes to many companies. I was not able to get a job interview because I had no fixed address. I was turned out of the studio. I was no longer a psychologist, just an ordinary man who owned the clothes I was wearing and nothing more. My thoughts were interrupted by the phone.

"My daughter needs you now. How much money do you require?" he came straight to the question of money; which was a shock to me.

"Could you give me prepayment!" I thought for a while and said.

"No problem," he said.

I had corresponded with him for two times, but I had never met him in the flesh. On Sunday morning I was woken by the cell phone.

"Have you received my advance payment?" he asked.

"Thank you. I have received your remittance." I said.

"Please notify me of the change of the office's address," he said.

"Sorry, I forgot. I'll text it to you." I said.

"Are you free today?" he asked.

"Your daughter can come at any time," I answered.

After a while, there came a rat-a-tat on the door. I turned the latch of the door and opened it so gently. I gave a start as she entered. She looked distraught and haggard.

"What's the matter with you?" I asked.

"Last night I relived my terrifying ordeal," she answered.

"You should see a doctor," I said.

"The doctor said it is not a physical problem," she said.

"Give me a sketch of your childhood," I said.

"Except for my illnesses, I had had a particularly happy childhood," she said.

"Could you be more specific?" I said.

We talked for hours and hours. I would have liked to ask questions, but I had moved on to another topic, "are you currently on any medication?"

"Yes, I am." she answered.

"What are all those medicines?" I asked.

"The doctor had cut me off from my medication. I dosed myself with sedative," she said.

"No need to take medicine for this illness," I said.

"Really?" she was dubious of my honesty.

"Please, believe me." I said.

Next day, she was in the best of humors.

"Thank you," she said.

"I had a good night's sleep and was feeling very full of beans." she added.

"May I go to school?" she asked.

"Of course," I answered.

"Great!" she was delirious with joy.

"Don't strain yourself too much," I added.

"What is your father?" suddenly I asked.

She didn't answer my question. This put me in a very awkward position. I pretended to cough a cry, "goodbye."

I zipped through all of the recruitment websites in a couple of days. I got the job interview on the first take and made it to the final round of applicants. Just then, my cell phone rang.

"Excuse me," I got up to leave.

It was followed by a familiar voice, "where are you now?"

"I am a little a bit busy right now, can we talk later?" I hung up the phone.

"Sorry," I returned to the interview room.

"We have narrowed it down to you and two other candidates," the interviewer said.

"Thank you," I said.

Just then my cell-phone rang again. I switched off my mobile phone.

"Please go back," the interviewer said.

I looked up and saw the interviewer, froze for a moment. I foreboded that I might fail.

"Goodbye," I stood up and went out.

Waiting for the result was torture. Two weeks went by with hardly a word from that company. I suffered continual her harassment. The harassment had become too much to tolerate and I decided to move out. And not long after that, I moved away from Dehradun and changed my mobile phone number. Like many fugitives, I lived in my home town unmolested for many days. I was once more jarred awake by the ringing cell phone.

"Hello," I rubbed my eyes.

"You think I couldn't find you as you changed your mobile number," Himani's father said.

"How do you know my mobile number?" I asked.

"It's nothing to do with you," he answered.

"Really?" I hung up the phone.

A few days later, I received a summons to appear in court. On the summons was written: I could not leave Dehradun; I was in debt for my rent.

2 CHAPTER RETURN TO DEHRADUN

I collected my belongings and left. I was wrongly accused. The feeling nagged at me. I returned to Dehradun. For some inexplicable reason, the landlord had dropped the charge. The girl had pined away dreadfully. I was moved with compassion.

"Your immune system would reject the transplanted organ as a foreign object," I said.

"What should I do?" she asked.

"I don't know," I said.

"How much do you know about the donor?" I asked.

"I don't know anything about the donor," she answered.

"You mean-" she looked at me.

"I'm a layman." I cut in.

"I see," she said, "could you help me?"

"What other options do I have?" I asked.

"Thank you," a faint smile played on her face.

"What should be the first step?" she asked.

"First, rent a house." I said.

"What do you mean?" she looked at me with doubt and alarm.

"Where shall I be staying?" I asked.

"I'm sorry. You will get double pay at the end of the month." she said.

"Thank you," I answered.

I was out of work at the time. The human nature was complicated, idiographic and changeful. She became my employer. She found the doctor in the hospital. The doctor clammed up when she mentioned the donor. She nearly went bonkers with frustration.

"Perhaps your father knows the donor," I said.

She said not a word, but nodded her head.

She went home and mapped out her strategy. "Do you know the donor?"

"Why do you ask me that?" her father looked at her.

She tried to speak, but for once, her voice had left her.

"You should ask to the doctor," her father said.

"You're right," she turned and left.

"What's the donor's name?" I asked.

"I don't know," she answered.

"Maybe you'd better tell me what this is all about," she said.

"I'm not Sherlock," I said.

"I employ you by paying not to let you sit," she said.

It left me at a complete loss for words.

"Why don't you speak?" she looked at me.

"We must infiltrate into the hospital," I said.

"Let's go," she grabbed my arm.

"Where are we going?" I asked.

"Hospital," she said.

She led the way to the hospital.

"Where is the medical-record department?" I asked.

"What's the number of your Aadhaar?" a woman asked.

I gave her a glance.

"I don't have Aadhaar," she answered.

"Sorry," the woman said.

I slid some notes into the woman's pocket.

"What do you want to know?" the woman asked.

My eyes turned to Himani. We looked in the files for an hour, but we drew a blank. The absence of clues baffled us.

"What should we do?" she asked.

"I don't know," I said.

My words made her heart burn with frustration.

"You'd better write your dream down from now on," I said to her.

"No problem," she turned and left.

A few days later, she visited me in my new apartment. She brought me a diary.

"Sit down, please." I said.

"Thank you," she looked around my room.

"You can play the guitar," she said.

"I am just started learning. Don't laugh at me." I said.

"Anything for drinks? I have tea and sprite." I asked.

"Tea," she answered.

She bowed slightly before taking her cup, "thank you."

I unfolded the diary and read it. My mind wouldn't stop going round and round on the same subject and I seemed to be getting nowhere. She was breathless with anticipation. I shook my head. She heaved a deep sigh.

"Sorry, I do try my best." I looked at her.

"How much will you pay me?" I asked.

"You want to leave?" she asked.

"Yes," I answered.

"I'll not give you any money," she said to me.

"Why? You must concede that I have tried my best." I said.

"I shall settle up with you at the end of the month," she said.

I realized that I had been taken for a ride, and had to accept the arrangement with resignation. I felt that one day seemed a year. My brain was continually on the rack about the means of living. In the middle of the night, the telephone rang.

"I have no money," I hung up the phone.

When I awoke, I found one text message. I received the remit money and sat up with a start.

I rubbed my eyes, read the text message again.

A ringing phone silenced me, "hello."

"I had a nightmare last night," she said.

She told the dream in the first person.

"Are you listening?" she suddenly asked.

For a long while I remained speechless.

"Are you still there?" she asked.

"I saw in you a mirror image of my younger self," I said.

She smiled and asked. "How old are you?"

I made no answer to her question, "you just need a listener."

"You're right," she thought a moment and then said.

"Why didn't you tell your father?" I asked.

After a moment's silence she went on speaking, "I didn't want to worry him."

"Is it true?" I asked.

"What do you mean by that?" she asked.

"Why do you like self-deception?" I asked.

She had severely disrupted my life. It seemed an appropriate opportunity to end, "the best doctor is yourself."

She was silent for a few seconds and said, "I want to see you."

"Where shall we meet?" I asked.

"I will text you the address," she said.

"OK," I hung up the phone.

A minute later I got a short message: South Asia Hotel.

I was stunned with by the sudden message.

The problem became even more complicated. I went round the streets and found the hotel. I went directly to her room and knocked on the door. To my surprise, the door was unlocked. After drawing the curtains, she slammed the door.

"What do you want to do?" I asked.

She whipped off her coat, revealing her scar. I felt too shocked to move.

"Can you feel my pain?" she asked.

"I'm sorry. Get your clothes on; hurry up!" I said.

This experience, however, though surprising was not extraordinary. The extraordinary thing was what happened three weeks later.

I withdrew to my rented room. After tossing and turning all night. I awoke before dawn to the clatter of something pelting the window. I splashed water on my face, then brushed my teeth brushed. Suddenly, an idea flashed into through my mind. I lifted my phone and dialled her number, "hello!"

"What's up?" she asked.

"It can't be expressed in a few words," I answered.

She appointed to meet me at the entrance of the restaurant.

"Sorry to have kept you waiting," I said.

Just then, my stomach rumbled emptily.

"Why don't you offer me a drink?" She asked. We entered the restaurant.

"What would you like to eat?" I asked.

"Suit yourself," she answered.

"How about the roast lamb with mint sauce?" I asked.

"Sounds good," she said.

I ordered a salad and a curry.

"This curry is too hot," I was so starving that I wolfed down a big bowl of curry.

"What do you want to see me about?" she asked.

"Oh, sorry," I dabbed at my lips with the napkin.

"Do you remember your dreams?" I asked.

"Oh aye, yeah." she said.

"Gun," I reminded her.

"What do you mean?" she looked at me.

"Criminal case," I answered.

"Are you kidding?" she asked.

"I know how you feel. This is only speculation." I said.

"Don't keep me guessing. Go on!" she said.

"This is the breakthrough," I said.

"Will you please have the bill ready for me," I raised my hand.

A waiter came along with an account book under his arm, "pay with cash or credit card?"

"Cash," I said.

I felt for my wallet and found it gone. I was surprised, to take a cold sweat.

"What's up?" she asked.

"I've lost my wallet," I whispered.

"Credit card," she handed a credit card to the waiter.

"Sorry," my face flushed scarlet.

"It doesn't matter," she said.

She and I left the restaurant.

"Do you have a goal?" she asked.

"No, I don't." I said.

"At least we have a range," I added.

She showed her teeth in a humourless grin. We walked on a little way without speaking. All at once I in advance stopped so suddenly that she caromed against me.

"What's wrong with you?" she complained.

"Shush," I said.

A man's furtive manner made me follow him.

"He stole my money," I said to her.

I caught up with the man and grabbed his arm, "give me my money back."

"I don't know you," he said.

"You stole my money," I said.

"Have you got any proofs?" he looked at me.

I tried to speak, but for once, my voice had left me.

"Sorry, we got the wrong person." she pulled on my arm.

He walked out of the alley with a self-confident swagger.

"Forget it," she penetrated my thought.

Searching for the clue was like trying to find a needle in a haystack. Nothing had resulted from my efforts. Her illness was being aggravated by anxieties.

I was used to having my sleep interrupted.

"You are a fraud," she said.

"What time is it now?" I banged down the phone. The next morning she telephoned me and gave me my notice.

"Thank you," I breathed a sigh of relief.

"What did you say?" she asked.

"I'll not give you any money," she added.

"I don't care," I answered.

"Where are you now?" she asked.

"Why should I tell you?" I hung up the phone.

After breakfast I ordered a taxi. I was anxious to go back home as I had been away for a very long time.

I glanced at my watch, "can you drive faster?"

"What time are you getting your train?" the taxi driver asked.

"11 o'clock," I said.

"Don't worry. You'll be on time." the taxi driver said to me.

Station staff announced the arrival of the train over the tannoy. A porter relieved me of the three large cases.

"Where are you going?" I was hailed by a voice which struck a familiar note.

"You should find a psychiatrist," I suggested.

She looked at my eyes. "Have you ever considered my feelings?"

I continued to walk, didn't look at her, kept my face forward.

"Do you have the business license?" she caught my arm.

"That's none of your business," I pushed her away.

"I'm afraid I have no alternative but to report you to the government," she said.

I hesitated, then stopped.

The waiting crowd formed up in a long line, "can't you be quicker!"

The train jolted into motion, leaving her on the platform. Suddenly, she felt a tap on her shoulder and turned to face me, and for a while we sat in silence. She ran into my arms. I was of a rational turn of mind. I shoved her out of the way. She was marvelously cool again, smiling as if nothing had happened.

"Have you eaten yet?" she broke the silence. The clock was striking twelve.

"Let's get some dinner," she said.

Obviously she had plenty of money and was generous in its use with being ostentatious.

"Where does your money come from?" my eyes ran over the sea of plates on the table.

"That doesn't concern you," she answered.

The only thing I could do is keep quiet and sit this one out.

"Aren't you hungry?" she asked.

"Oh, I forget." I picked up my knife and fork.

I looked up to see the thief and another man standing in the doorway. I looked down at the floor and the smile died on my lips.

"What's wrong?" she looked at me.

"Don't look back," I brought out my cell phone. The thief filched some notes from a woman's wallet and slid the wallet into her pocket. I followed at a discreet distance. I followed the thief up the street but somewhere in the large crowd I let him slip. I turned and found a short, stocky man in shirt-sleeves standing behind me.

"I saw you in the restaurant," I said.

He biffed me one on the head. When I opened my eyes I saw a nurse with a thermometer standing at the end of my bed.

"Where am I now?" I developed an appalling headache.

"You should rest, not talk so much." said Himan.

"Sorry to have troubled you," I said.

"It's nothing," Himan answered.

Suddenly, she gave me a roguish smile.

"What's wrong?" I looked at her.

Himan's eyes wandered restlessly around my hospital gown, "it may make you smarter."

I tried to answer, but there was no word. There seemed to be some subtle connection between her and me. We knew it without saying it. Days passed, and I started to rally.

"Thank you, I am perfectly recovered." I said to Himan.

"You have got quite well!" she looked at me in surprise.

I felt puzzled at her reply, "what's wrong with you?"

"Goodbye," she waved her hand and left.

"Hi," I shouted. "Where are you going?"

Just then, the door opened and a nurse stepped in.

"You may be able to leave hospital tomorrow," the nurse said to me.

"Thank you," I allowed myself a wry smile.

"Aren't you glad?" the nurse looked at me.

"You misunderstand me. I'm very glad!" I smiled and said.

"I feel a little uncomfortable, dizziness, want to sleep." I added.

"Okay, I won't keep you any longer." the nurse shrugged her shoulders.

I breathed a sigh of relief. Suddenly the door opened again and the nurse came in.

"Excuse me," she said. "Please do not leave the hospital before being formally discharged."

"No problem," I smiled and said.

When she'd gone, I tidied away my possessions. I swapped the hospital gown for my clothes. When I pushed the door open, the nurse was sitting bolt upright in the nurse's station. Luckily, she didn't see me. My head had been withdrawn like lightning.

I sucked in deep lungful of air.

I stepped back from the door and glanced over my shoulder and saw the sheet. My sickroom was on the second floor. I tied the sheet into a bundle. I evaded nurse by climbing through a window and shinning down a drainpipe.

"Hey," a security guard asked. "What are you doing?"

"I didn't do anything," I flicked the dust from my suit.

"Catch him," the nurse poked out her head and shouted.

I ran faster than I had ever run in my life. I glanced at a car's rear mirror. A line was beginning to form. I looked down at my feet and the smile died on my lips. On my feet I wore big slippers, like old bags. I found that the pursuers were close at my heels. Crossing the street was a vegetable fair. I was wet with sweat and took off my clothes. They barged through the crowd. I failed to negotiate a bend and ran into a cow.

"Sorry, sorry." I zoomed through junctions without stopping and sped the wrong way down a one-way street, hotly pursued by two security men. I went out the vegetable fair and walked a quarter of a mile to the railroad tracks. I heard the train coming and crossed the railroad track in one leap. Despite both hunger and fatigue, I traveled forward. I glanced back over the path I had come. The path was nearly empty.

"Thank goodness!" I said with a sigh of relief.

I flopped, exhausted, on to the ground. I took my cell phone out of my trouser pocket and dialled her number.

"Where are you now?" I asked.

She banged down the telephone.

"Damn," I yelled at the top of my voice.

I thought of my coat and returned to the vegetable fair. I tried to find it, but had no success. Just then, my stomach rumbled emptily. I smelled the delicious odor of cooked meat. I took a sip of saliva to moisten my dry throat. I forced myself to subdue and overcome my appetite. Suddenly, an awful scream singed the sky. The scream froze me again. A hush fell over the crowd and I knew something terrible had happened. I took a deep breath and joined the flow of people. I was shocked by what I saw. A boy was pinned under the car.

"What's the matter with him?" I asked.

"He stole a brioche," a middle-aged man answered.

"What do they want to do?" I asked.

"They want to break his arm," the middle-aged man explained.

"This is against the law," I said.

I dragged the boy away from the car.

"What are you doing?" a man said and held on to my arm.

"What is the value of the brioche?" I asked.

The man looked at me and looked down. I pulled off my sopping belt and handed it to him, "is it enough?"

A glimmer of amusement showed in the man's eyes. The crowd, which had gathered to watch the fun, dispersed.

"Thank you," the boy extended his hand.

"It doesn't matter," I hitched up my trousers, which were rather loose.

"How can I repay you?" he silently held my hand.

"You are so polite," I said.

"Please excuse me for a little while, I want to do something." the boy said.

"Oh, you're busy." I said.

"Goodbye," the boy turned and left.

I waved to the boy. In a moment my watch was gone.

"Hey, give me my watch back." I shouted.

The boy had vanished in the crowd. I was beyond regarding self-respect, weighed down by fatigue and wretchedness. I crouched on the ground and felt a current of cool air blowing in my face. I suddenly saw a wallet. This was the wallet which I was looking for. There was only a credit card in my wallet. I picked up my trousers and hurried to the bank. I had a very high limit on my credit card. I solved one problem and another would immediately pop up, "where should I put these banknotes?"

Just then, my cell phone rang. I looked down at the cell phone number in undisguised disgust. I hung up the phone. Money was not everything, but without money one can go hardly anywhere. I had new clothes, a new hairstyle-the whole caboodle. I ate a great big dinner and withdrew to my rented room. I recognized her at a glance.

"Why are you here?" I made no attempt to conceal my dislike of her.

She showed her teeth in a humourless grin.

"What are you smiling at?" I asked.

"I read my father's diary. The donor's name is Bill Singh." she said.

"What does all this have to do with me?" I asked.

"Money," she answered.

"I do not trust you," I said.

"Cash," she looked at my eyes.

I thought the best way to deal with a tease is to ignore her.

"You can leave here now," I pushed the door open.

"I promise to pay you double time," she said.

"Would you go? Come on, you're insulting me." I said to her.

"Triple wages," she said.

I slammed the door.

"What if you can't pay the bank back in a month?" she said.

"What do you want me to do?" I opened the door and asked.

She glanced at me with a pleased smile.

A few days later I dialled her phone. "He didn't live Dehradun."

"How do you know that?" she asked.

"It has nothing to do with you," I answered.

She hung up the phone. I tried to reach her, but the line was busy. She had been like that for days, silent and aloof. It would come as a rude shock when my salary cannot be cashed. As time went by, I could live no longer. Directly after lunch I was packed and ready to go. Just then, my cell phone sounded.

"Where are you now?" her voice was low and urgent.

"What's up?" I asked.

"I want to see you now," she said.

A sudden sharp knock on the door startled me.

"Would you like to tell me what happened?" I opened the door.

"May I come in?" she asked.

"Please," I closed the door.

"My father found me stealing his diary," she said.

"So what?"

"He wanted to send me back to school," she was pale and nervous.

"What can I do for you?" I asked.

"Find the donor's family," she said.

"Is it necessary?" I looked at her.

She opened an envelope and fanned out a stack of new five hundred rupees.

"Could you give me some details?" I asked.

She shook her head. I gave a wry smile. The silence was broken only by the tick of the clock. Suddenly, I had a brainwave, "let's go!"

"Where are we going?" she asked.

I reached the restaurant and thrust my way through it. I wiped the sweat off my face and looked around. Time passed, and still he did not appear.

"Who are you looking for?" she asked.

My mind went totally blank. I wandered aimlessly around the streets.

"What the heck are you doing?" she caught my arm.

"You interrupted my train of thought," I said.

"I'm tired. I want to rest for a while." she said.

"I'm here to help you," I turned and looked at her.

"I'm hungry," she gave an oblique look to one side. There was a new snack at the corner of the street. In a very short time I was dragged right up to the snack's door.

"You will pay the bill this time because last time I did it," she said.

"I want a hamburger, a large coke and a cake." she said to a waiter.

"But-" I was about to speak when the waiter handed me a bill.

I was speechless at that time.

"You are not a stingy man, right?" she smiled and said.

I watched as she got a tray and sat at a position that beside the window.

"Aren't you hungry?" she chewed a mouthful of hamburger.

I did not answer her question. I drew the thief from memory.

"What are you doing?" she asked.

I stared thoughtfully into the distance, deliberating the state of affairs. Her eyelids drooped and she yawned, "what time is it now?"

"18:29," I answered.

"Let's go home," she stood up.

"Where is your home?" I asked.

"Your home," she grinned at me in unashamed delight.

She took my arm and walked towards my home. She fell back on the bed and at once fell asleep. I held my anger in check. She turned over onto her back and began to snore. I stretched out on the sofa and kicked off my

shoes. I could not relax and still felt wide awake. I slowly sat up on the sofa
and calculated the cost of the journey.

Suddenly, I heard a muffled cough behind me.

"What are you doing?" she asked.

"Did you sleep well?" I took off my spectacles.

"I had a dream again," she said.

"Aren't you curious about what I dreamed about?" she asked.

"When you snore, I can hear you in the next room," I said to her.

"Sorry," she looked at me, "does my snoring bother you?"

I turned around and put out my hand to turn off the light.

"Hey, are you angry?" she leaned forward and patted me on the shoulder.

"Not at all," I explained. "I think I'm getting a bit drowsy."

"You got a minute?" she asked.

"I'm mad," I closed my eyes, covered my face.

She was on the point of saying something when her cell phone rang.

It was followed by a familiar voice, "where are you now?"

She had rung off before he could press her for an answer.

"You are so arrogant that no one will like you," I raised my head and said.

"What's it to you?" she growled.

She turned her back to me. The air seemed to be frozen. I could not help
having compassion for the poor girl.

A ray of sunlight pierced the window. I rubbed the sleep out of my eyes,
"what time is it now?"

She left long ago. I began packing up my things and gave the owner of flat
my notice. I had no choice but to turn back. A cool breeze made the heat
pleasantly bearable. I went to the railway station by bus. When I went to the
railway station, a large crowd of people had gathered. I composed myself,
then walked on unhurriedly. Suddenly, I felt two tiny arms wrap around my
leg.

"Why are you here?" I asked.

"Please," the boy was on his stomach, his legs splayed apart.

"What's the matter with you?" I looked at his legs.

"I was knocked over by a car and broke my legs," the boy answered.

"You want to cheat me? It's no go!" I pushed him away.

I pulled my leg free, and strode for the railway station.

"Your watch," the boy shouted.

I turned around and saw him, froze for a moment. He crept along on his hands and knees.

"Here you are," the boy handed the watch back to me.

I was full of sympathy for him, yet I didn't know what to say.

"It's time for you to go," the boy broke the silence.

"Please wait on, will you? I'm just coming!" I ran for a restaurant and up the steps, taking them two at a time.

"Please pack the dish in a doggie bag," I said to a waiter.

When I returned there, I found the boy gone. I remained silent all along, standing there woodenly. Just then my cell phone rang.

"Where are you now?" Himani's father asked.

"What's up?" I asked.

"Where is my daughter?" he asked.

"I don't know," I answered.

"Please help me, I entreat you." he said.

I was moved with sympathy, "I'll contact her."

"Thank you," he hung up the phone.

I dialled her number, "your father is waiting for you at home. You'd better go back right now."

"I don't want to live anymore," she said.

"Where are you now?" I quickly inquired.

"South Asia Hotel," she answered.

"Wait at hotel for me," I said.

I rushed to my destination without a single halt. When I saw her, she smiled and waved.

"I'm tired of this hotel. Let's settle up and go." she flicked a crumb off the corner of her mouth.

"Ask the waiter for the bill; I want to go home," she said.

I hesitated for a moment, for I wondered whether she had the ability to repay me. Just then, my cell phone rang.

"Hello," I picked up my cell phone.

"Have you found my daughter?" he asked.

"She stands beside me now," I answered.

"Could I possibly have a word with my daughter?" he said.

"Of course," I turned with a little nod and watched her walk away.

"Hi, where are you going?" I shouted.

The waiter burst in when I was going to leave, "check, please!"

I felt cheated and put-upon and left the hotel in a huff. She had disappeared without a trace. I had already missed my train, "I couldn't just let her make a fool of me."

I suddenly saw her in the distance. I put on a spurt and soon caught her up.

"I order you to halt," I called.

She swivelled round to face me, "do you want to see me about something?"

"Sorry, I got the wrong person." I said, a little embarrassed.

A ringing phone silenced me.

"Where is my daughter now?" Himani's father asked.

"She managed to sneak in through the door while I wasn't looking," I said.

"Where are you now?" he answered.

"South Asia Hotel," I blurted out.

"Wait a moment, I'll be right there." he hung up the phone.

I had to walk back two miles. I could hear my stomach roaring and had a bite at a food stall. Just then my cell phone rang.

"I'm in the South Asia Hotel. Where are you now?" Himani's father asked.

"Please wait a moment," I began to have trouble with my belly.

"What's up?" he asked.

"I ate myself sick," I explained.

"Where is the toilet?" I hung up the cell phone.

"There are no proper toilets, but only an outdoor latrine," a passer-by answered.

"Where is it?" I asked.

"Just over there," the passer-by said.

"Thank you," I said.

I caught get a glimpse of the thief's face as I ran past. He stared at me, thunderstruck. As the situation became risky, the guy turned tail and fled.

"Halt," I shouted.

His pace quickened as I approached him. I crossed between the traffic to the far side of the street. He cleared a passage for himself through the crammed streets and vanished into the haze near the horizon. I immediately crumpled to the ground. Already I was sweating as the sun beat down upon me. I lifted the phone and dialled her number, "your father is looking for you."

"I see," she said.

"Don't hang up, please!" I cut in.

"I want to see you," I said.

"Where are you now?" she asked.

"I'll text it to you," I said.

After a while, she presented herself before me.

"Do you want to see me about something?" she looked at me.

After a long period of hesitation, I finally called her farther, "I find your daughter."

She snatched my cell phone from my hand and flung it to the ground.

"What are you doing?" I picked up my cell phone.

"Oh, shit! It's broken." I complained.

She gave me an envelope.

"It's not about the money," I said.

"You don't like it?" she asked.

I grabbed the envelope. She glanced at me with a pleased smile. I turned to look at her.

"What are you driving at?" I asked calmly.

"Find the donor's family," she said.

"We need to find the thief," I added.

"Why?"

"Clue," I answered.

I led her through the streets to the railway station. It took me some time to find the boy.

"Have you eaten?" I asked.

The boy shook his head.

"Let's go," I picked up the boy.

"Who is he?" she whispered.

I was well into work and not inclined to conversation. After a time we came to a restaurant. The boy polished off a large steak, salad, broccoli swimming in thick sauce.

"I've had enough, thank you." the boy said.

I took out a portrait-painting from my bag, "do you know him?"

"No, I don't." the boy answered.

I had been very depressed and upset about this whole situation.

"Don't give up," she patted me on the shoulder.

"Can you have the check?" I said to her.

The boy didn't tell me where he lived, and I took him the railway station. I waved goodbye and went up the steps. I could spy on him a window without being seen. The late afternoon sun brightened the interior of the railway station. A stranger walked up to the boy and took him into a van. I rushed out of the railway station and hurried away to hail a taxi. We followed the van up the street but somewhere in the large crowd we let it slip. The boy didn't show up the next day, and, despite our efforts to find him, by the next week he was still missing. We were in a fix. We wandered up and down the road aimlessly.

"It's boiling in here," complained Himani.

"We ought not to be quarrelling now," I said.

"You were busy all day and achieved nothing," she said.

"Then what is your good idea?" I asked.

She remained silent for some time.

I stopped for a moment, and then passed on.

"Hi," she shouted, "wait for me."

As I walked forward I could feel cobwebs brushing my face.

"If we keep on our way for another hour we should reach the slum," she said.

"Oh good," I said.

"Are you mad?" she looked at me in surprise.

"You can stay here if you like," I said to her.

"What exactly do you mean?" she shouted.

"You are trying to find some excuse to start a quarrel," I said.

An hour later we reached the slum. The houses were in a dilapidated condition and seemed as if they would collapse at any moment. The streets were filthy and choked with exhaust fumes. I turned to look inside a house in a reflex action.

"What do you want to do?" an old woman asked.

"Do you know him?" I took out the portrait-painting.

The old woman shook her head.

"Is there a disabled boy near here?" I continued.

"What do you do?" the old woman asked.

"I'm his friend," I blurted out.

"Do you know him? Could you please tell me where he is?" I begged.

"His room number is 2009," the old woman said.

"Thanks," I turned and left.

3 CHAPTER LOOK FOR 2009

A spot of rain fell on my hand. It never rains but it pours. We were wet all over like two drowned rats and ran to the nearest hotel and booked a room. I thought of the envelope.

"What are you looking for?" she asked.

"Do you see the envelope?" I asked.

"It's in my jacket pocket," she answered.

"Why?"

"Did you find the donor's family?" she asked.

"You," I stared at her, now wordless.

The rain stopped and the sky cleared up. We separated. I returned to the slum. My thoughts jumbled and raced like children fighting. The ground was still very muddy. Then I realized I was cheated and the room number was fake. She had no intention of paying the cash. Suddenly, a group of young men surrounded me.

"What are you doing?" a tall young man asked.

"I'm looking for 2009," there was a nervous edge to my voice.

Their laughter filled the air.

"Are you a cop?" the tall young man's face suddenly turned solemn, his voice confidential.

"I swear to god! I'm not a cop." I said.

"Who can prove it?" the tall young man asked.

I took out my watch, "it is my friend's watch. And I feel that he may live somewhere around here."

"What did that person look like?" the tall young man asked.

"I don't remember. He is a cripple." I said.

The tall young man exchanged a knowing look with his mates. I was led to a fenced enclosure. A broken small old grey house came into sight.

"He's in there," the tall young man said.

I said thanks, then they turned and walked off without another word. I opened the door and went in.

"You live here!" I looked at the boy.

I peered slowly around the small crowded house. Books were scattered around the room.

"Are these all yours?" I asked.

"Yes, they are." the boy answered.

"You're great!" I couldn't help noticing that he coloured slightly.

"Have you eaten yet?" I asked.

The boy shook his head.

"Wait for me," I turned and left.

I soon returned from the restaurant with a bowl of Rogan josh. That boy walked into the meal as if he hadn't seen food for a week.

"Eat slowly and don't gobble!" I took out chicken curry and rice, and naan bread.

"The naan bread was so good that I scoffed the lot," the boy said.

"Aren't you hungry?" the boy asked abruptly.

"I'm not hungry," I said.

"My stomach is completely full. Thank you a thousand times, you're an angel. What can I do for you?"

"Do you know him?" I took out the portrait-painting.

The harmony in the room had dissipated.

"Let me say it again. I don't know him." the boy said.

"Do you know it?" I took out my watch.

"What do you mean?" he looked at me.

The door was suddenly flung open. The tall young man came in with a cigarette dangling from the corner of his mouth. "What are you doing?"

"I gave the watch to him," I said in defence.

The tall young man darted a glance at the boy. He didn't say a word.

"No news is good news," the tall young man turned and left.

I sighed with inward relief, "I must say goodbye to you."

I got away as quick as I could. I didn't return to the hotel. All my convictions deserted me. I had a strong desire to reach to my hometown. I had a poor sense of direction and soon got lost. I left the slum and finally reached the railway station after passing through many places. Suddenly I realized I'd left my money at the hotel. I returned to the hotel.

"Did you find the donor's family?" asked Himani.

"Do you want to give me the envelope?" I asked.

"What do you base this conclusion on?" she looked at me.

I caught sight of my wallet in a mirror, "give me your cell phone."

"Why?"

I snatched the cell phone from her hand.

"Hey, where are you going?" she said.

I missed the last bus; I had to take a taxi. I finally arrived at the railway station, but I didn't get the ticket. I was going to have to spend the night here whether I liked it or not. It made me so sad when I saw young people begging or sleeping rough on the streets. The sun had already set, leaving the sky afire with orange and green light. At this moment a van stopped at a young man. It was evident that he had not fulfilled the task. The young man had been beaten and humiliated by them. He was left shouting abuse as the van sped off. I watched him from a shadowy corner.

"What are you looking at?" he shouted.

"It's none of your business," I replied.

He turned his anger on me. The young man grabbed my collar and we tussled over that. He screamed at me to 'stop it' as we struggled on the ground.

"Do you know him?" he pointed at the portrait-painting.

"Yes, I do." I gathered up my things that were scattered around the ground.

"What's up?" I said to him.

"Nothing much," he answered.

I gave a wry smile. Then I remembered my stolen credentials, which cheered me up.

"Where is he now?" I asked.

"I don't know," he answered.

I reached into my wallet and took out one of the bills. Gradually, a smile appeared on his face. I went round the streets and found the thief's abode. He answered the door as soon as I knocked.

"Why are you here?" he felt numb with horror.

He pushed me away and I fell back on the ground. In a moment he was gone. I rummaged through his abode but still could not find them.

"I mistake him?" I said to myself.

Just then, the cell phone rang. I heard the familiar voice, but tuned out the words.

"What did you say?" I asked.

"Where is my daughter now?" Himani's father asked.

"She booked a room in a hotel not far from the slum," I answered.

"Tell me the address," Himani's father said.

"Oh, where is my pen?" he said. "Wait a second."

"Don't worry," I said.

The door was kicked open with a bang. A crowd surrounded me, "who are you?"

"Stop talking rubbish," then I heard footsteps: someone sprinting towards me from behind. I turned and found a short, stocky man in shirt-sleeves standing behind me. He bashed me on the head. The pain was so bad that I lost all sensation. The first I knew about it was when I woke up in the prison. Above me, in a niche on the wall, sat a tiny veiled Ganesh, the elephant god.

"Nice to see you again," he smiled and said.

"Sorry, I misunderstood you," I said.

"You misunderstood me," he laughed.

"How do I address you?" I asked.

Just then, the cell phone rang.

"Wait a minute," I picked up the cell phone.

"Where are you now?" asked Himani.

"I don't know," I answered.

The man grabbed the cell phone and dropped it to the ground. I was dumbstruck. We had not spoken to each other since. The prison was locked on the outside. I was curled up in a ball. I was uncertain about their intentions. I began a hunger strike to protest at my conditions. They tried not to take any notice at first but then they were offended by it. Those bullies beat me up. I gave up the attempt in despair. I was not an isolated example. When I was locked up in the prison, I found myself isolated from the outer world. I had resigned myself to fate. I was getting thinner every day and had nothing of use to them. They threw me into a brook. The small brook nearly dried up. It was full of flotsam and refuse. I felt myself slipping into unconsciousness.

I awoke from my sleep in a cold sweat. Dogs and little children romped happily in the brook. They saw me at once, and ran over to rescue me. The little children took six men and brought me into a farmhouse. The farmhouse had fallen into a state of dilapidation. I ran my tongue around my lips.

"Wait a moment, I'll get you some water." a man said.

I took a big gulp and almost chocked. He patted me gently on the back.

"Thank you. Do you have any food in your fridge?" I asked.

The man gave a wry smile, "just wait for a moment. I'm coming soon."

I was sorry for my words. The only food I ever got was the family's leftovers. I was so starving that I wolfed down a big bowl of rice.

"Thank you. My stomach is completely full." I covered my mouth with my hand and belched discreetly.

"These are not enough!" the man shoved the food into my mouth.

"Stop," I shouted.

"What do you want to do?" I asked.

He gave me a crooked grin. I saw a jagged scar ran through his belly.

"What's this?" I asked.

"This scar is from the bite of a dog," he answered.

"You are lying," I said.

"You got that right," all of a sudden this dude was all up on me. I shoved him out of the way and out of the door. This village looked a bit weird. The villagers looked gingerish. I stared at the strangers in horror. I escaped the village but was rushed to hospital suffering from shock. The only snag was that I had no money. I was yanked out of hospital. I felt completely in the dark on this matter. I didn't have relatives to return to are left to wander the streets and sleep rough. The mere mention of food had triggered off hunger pangs. Hunger made me hallucinate. The mist had been replaced by a kind of haze that seemed to amplify the heat. I desperately needed money. I approached every friend and acquaintance for help in vain and I was at my wit's end. I fell ill because of homesickness. I hadn't got a cent. I felt like a scrap collector trying to beg for a few bucks. I was suffering from acute sunstroke, starvation and exhaustion. I felt dizzy and suffocated. I came round in hospital and did not know where I was. Everything was a complete blank.

"Why am I here?" I thought.

Suddenly, I heard a familiar voice.

"You are-" I looked at him.

"I'm Himani's father," he hesitated, then offered his hand. I took it, but held it for only a moment.

"Do you find your daughter?" I asked.

He shook his head.

"Where is she now?" he asked.

"I don't know," I answered.

I stared at him for a moment, his face registering disbelief. "I'm not lying."

"I need to know what you were doing during that time," he said.

"I had been searching for the donor's family."

"Where are they now?" his voice was low and urgent.

"I have still not fully recovered," I reminded him.

"Sorry," he turned and left.

My condition was improving day by day. I was already walking normally and doing remedial exercise. About ten o'clock, I was aroused from my sleep by a knocking at the door.

"You are expected to be released from hospital today," Himani's father said.

I was silent for a few seconds.

"Aren't you glad?" he asked.

"I haven't got a cent," I said.

"You can rest assured that everything will be all right," he smiled and said.

"Thank you," I sighed with inward relief.

"Wait till I come back. I will not be long." he said.

I gazed affectionately after his receding figure. I was bored and desired to go for a walk. I opened the door and went out. The ICU caught my eyes when I padded the corridor.

I looked around and sniffed. "This place badly needs a decorator."

I pushed the door open and went in to the room. There was a lad lying on the bed. I picked up the medical record card and glanced through it. He was in a coma and on a life-support machine. Suddenly, the door of the room opened and a nurse stepped inside.

"What are you doing?" the nurse asked.

"Sorry, I go into the wrong room without realizing it." I turned and returned to my room.

"Where have you been?" Himani's father asked.

"I went to the restroom," I answered.

"The doctor allowed you to leave the hospital," he said. "You pack your trunk to go north, we leave for lunch."

The silver plated caster on the dining table caught my attention. A stand for cruets containing various condiments. On the table in front of me was a menu listing what I was about to eat. He ordered another bottle of champagne and poured a little more bourbon into his glass.

"Congratulations," he picked up his glass.

I gave the champagnes the once-over.

"Don't you like the Champagne?" he asked.

"Sorry, I don't drink." I answered.

"It doesn't matter," he smiled and said.

"What do you do?" I asked.

He thought for a moment and said," I'm a businessman."

I inclined my head very slightly.

"What's up?" he smiled and asked.

"Nothing much," I answered.

"You are out of hospital, but you can't go back to work." he said abruptly.

"Why?"

"I need you to look for my daughter," he said.

"No problem," I answered.

"How are they?" he asked abruptly.

"Who?" I looked at him.

"The donor's family," he said.

"They moved house without leaving a forwarding address."

"Oh, I see." he said to me.

We walked out of the restaurant and drew a blank in our search for Himani.
It bewildered and depressed him.

"I have an idea," I told him my plan.

We went to the bank to freeze her bank account. Soon his cell phone rang.
He looked at me pretty curious and smiling a little. I snatched his cell phone
from his hand and hung up the phone.

"What are you doing?" he asked.

"I accompany you home," I said.

He looked at me in blank amazement. As soon as he got home, the door
bell rang. I opened the door and stuck my head out.

"Why are you here?" she shouted.

"He is our guest," he said.

"So what?" she said.

"He found the donor's family," her father said.

"Really!" she looked at me.

I nodded my head.

"Where are they now?" she caught my arm.

"They moved house," I answered.

"You are fooling me again," she said.

"I'm not lying," I answered.

"Take me there," she grabbed my arm.

She dragged me from her home and hurried away to hail a taxi.

"Where are you going?" the taxi driver asked.

She directed a brief glance towards me.

"Go straight ahead," I said to the driver.

"Where on earth can they be?" she was beginning to get a bit ratty and fed up. "Do you have their phone number?"

"They don't have a phone," I said.

"Are you kidding?" she looked at me.

"Parking," I said to the taxi driver.

"What's up?" she asked.

"Not far, just ahead." I got off the taxi.

She was impatient as the first hour passed and then another. We returned to the slum again.

"Where on earth can they be?" she asked.

My anger finally overflowed, "you are too selfish."

"What did you say!" she shouted.

I clapped a hand over her mouth and pulled her aside. My grip slackened on her mouth.

"What do you want to do?" she asked.

"Shush," I said.

Just then a man came along. I went round to the off side of the wall.

"Who is he?" she whispered.

"I don't know him," I answered.

"How could you? Frighten me to jump!" she patted me on the head.

"No clue to his whereabouts has been found," I got straight to the point.

"Sorry," I said to her.

She asked me what I intended, but I wouldn't tell her. She delved into her rucksack and pulled out an envelope.

"What do you mean by that?" I looked at her.

"You deserved it," she handed the envelope to me.

"Thanks," I said.

I was just going to leave the slum when she latched on to my arm

"Would you like to stay and have dinner?"

I wrinkled my brows in concentration.

"Suppose we meet somewhere for a drink? I'll pay. How's that?" She added.

"Come on," she grabbed my arm.

I was led to an upper- scale restaurant. A waiter offered her the menu. She frowned at me anxiously.

"Let's go Dutch," I said to her.

"Oh, great!" she smiled and said.

"Are you ready to order?" the waiter asked.

She nodded her head. Food was placed before us, but she had little hunger for it.

"What's the matter with you?" I asked.

"I want to go to the restroom." she turned and left.

When she had not returned an hour later, I realized that I had been taken for a ride. When I opened the envelope, I was stunned, "there's only an empty envelope with nothing in it."

The eyes of the restaurant were now on me. I went directly to the reception, "I forgot to take my cell phone. May I use your phone?"

The waiter handed me his phone.

"Thank you," I lifted the phone and dialled her father's number.

"I need your help," I said.

"Where are you now?" Himani's father asked.

"What's your address?" I asked the waiter.

"Give me the phone," the waiter said.

Himani's father was on the scene in minutes, "tell me what happened."

I sketched the story briefly, telling the facts just as we had happened. He looked at me and laughed. I was red with shame. He waved at the waiter, who rushed to the table, "I want to check out, please. Will you please have the bill ready for me?"

At last, he gave the waiter a fat tip.

"That's certainly very generous of you," I said.

"Do you mind telling me where you think you're going?" he asked.

"I want to go home," I said.

He took a glance at his watch, "It's too late. You can put up my home for the night."

"Don't you worry about your daughter?" I asked.

"She'll be back," he said quietly.

It was dark by the time we got his home.

"This is all I have," he pushed the door open.

It was pitch-dark in the room and I couldn't see a thing, "why don't you turn on the light?"

"The electricity had been cut off," he took out his flashlight.

"God is always fair," I blurted out.

"What did you say?" he asked.

"I said nothing," I felt myself blush.
"The food in the freezer had thawed," he turned to look inside the freezer in a reflex action.
"Have you eaten yet?" he turned around and asked.
I couldn't withhold my laughter.
"Oh, I forget." he said.
Just then, I found all the streetlights came on.
"Oh, great!" he turned on the light.
Suddenly there came a rat-a-tat on the door.
"Your daughter," I said.
He gave me a knowing smile. He opened the door and his daughter went in.
"Get out," she shouted.
"This time you've gone too far," he stared at his daughter angrily.
"She is still a child." I said to him.
It was with an accent of severity that he continued, "you must apologise for your outrageous behaviour."
"Oh, forget it." I changed the topic. "Is that your bird?"
She turned away and cut me dead. I approached the birdcage. The bird stretched out its neck and ruffled its neck feathering.
"Himani," her father said, "you give up your room to the guest."
"I don't agree," she shouted.
His face clouded.
After a while, she came up to me. Her face was unmoved, but on her lips there was a trace of displeasure, "your bath is ready."
"Thank you," I smiled and said.
"The water is much too hot," I said.
I heard sounds of laughter in the next room. After the bath, I felt completely refreshed. My eyelids drooped and I yawned. I opened the door and went into her room. I peered slowly around the small crowded room. There were a single bed, a desk, a chair and a wardrobe in her bedroom.
"The bed is too narrow! Why doesn't he buy a bigger house?" I said.
I closed my eyes and fell asleep. Suddenly, I felt the bed was rocking.
"Where are my shoes?" I noticed that my slippers had disappeared.
"They are here," I was startled when she popped up at the door all smiles.
"Go out," I slammed the door.
"The bed is too small," I slept on the floor.
I fell straight into a dreamless sleep. Suddenly, I felt a tug at my shirt sleeve,

"who are you?"

A head bobbed up from under the bed. The little boy had his back towards me. I put on my glasses and began to gaze fixedly at the person.

"It's just a doll," I heaved a deep sigh.

Just then, the doll swivelled his head to look at me. The sound of my own screaming woke me up. I put on the light by the bed. I glanced over my shoulder and saw a statue watching me. I was so scared that I broke out in a cold sweat. Suddenly the clock struck twelve. I made a dive for the door, but the desk was in my way. I was stumbled down and torn the skin from my knees. I gave a sudden cry of pain and limped off her bedroom.

"What's the matter with you?" Himani patted my shoulder gently.

"You did give me a scare. Where is the water? I'm very thirsty." I said.

She went into the kitchen and opened the fridge.

"Thank you," I accepted the beer but what I wanted more than anything else was a cup of water. I upended the beer, and swallowed.

I felt wide awake, "why don't you go to bed now?"

"I had a nightmare tonight, and lost sleep." she answered.

I rubbed the back of my neck and smiled ruefully at her.

"What is this?" I asked abruptly.

"This is my father's diary," she answered.

"Does he know?" I said.

She raised her hand, and made a short, quick movement toward the right, "his snore disturbed my sleep."

I looked at her and smiled.

"How can you be so vindictive?" I asked abruptly.

"I don't know," her eyes stared into mine with an expression of absolute honesty.

"I see," I said.

"What do you understand?" she smiled and asked.

I evaded her eyes and fell into silence. She turned her focus to her father's diary.

"Exactly what are you looking for?" I asked.

"My father is a participant. By the way, my father has the habit of keeping a diary, half in Hindi, half in English."

"What have you found so far?" I asked.

She let out her breath in a long sigh and shook her head.

Just then, the light went out.

"Why, the electricity is off!" she said.

The ultraviolet lamp became the only illuminant.

"It is light enough to read," she said.

"I'm certain that this lamp set will operate on batteries," I said.

"Rubbish," she grunted.

She let go with a sudden yell.

"Shush!" I shushed me with a forefinger to the lips.

"What's this?" she handed the diary to me.

I made out three dim numbers in the dark.

"What does '123' mean?" she looked at me.

"I don't know," I answered.

She snatched the diary out of my hand and leafed through it. The diary bombarded all of her with words of sex.

"He's way out of line," she roared.

"What's up?" I asked.

She gave me a factual account of the chronology of his brief liaison.

"This is human nature," I said.

She turned back to that page.

"Maybe it is a hotel's room number," I said.

"I don't think it possible," she said. "It was recorded on that period."

"I'm afraid I don't understand you. What's the point?" I asked.

"He stayed with me at that period," she answered.

"This confirms what I suspected all along," she added.

Dawn was beginning to show in the east. I stretched my arms out and gave a great yawn, "you think too much."

"What would I do?" she asked.

"Go to bed. You look tired out." I said, "give me the diary."

"No," she said.

"You're going to be a good girl now," I said.

She turned a deaf ear to my advice. I grabbed the diary and we tussled over that. At this juncture his bedroom door opened.

"What are you doing?" he asked.

I realized that her body was curled beneath me in a foetal position.

"You must have misunderstood," I raised my head and said.

She gave a sudden cry of pain and put her hand to her heart.

"Let her go," he ordered.

My mind went totally blank.

"Get out," he shouted.

I huddled on my clothes and left their home. I composed myself as best as I could. I was feeling guilty and depressed, repentant and scared. I nerved myself to face the question. I returned to her home and knocked and a policeman opened the door to me. I was shocked so much that I froze.

"Is he the man to whom you referred?" the policeman asked.

She nodded her head.

"I need you to come with us," the policeman said to me.

The policeman exchanged a knowing look with his colleague. I was led to the police station. The policeman handed me a pen and some blank paper.

"What do you want me to write about?" I asked.

"How did you meet each other?" the policeman asked.

I was just about to speak when the policeman stopped me, "write down." Scene after scene of past events reappeared in my mind. My thoughts flowed easily; I felt a sense of joy in the composition.

"Is that all?" the policeman asked.

I gave a nod of assent.

"What is your demand?" he asked.

"Is it possible I'll phone my parents?" I said.

The policeman thought for a moment and then approved.

I bowed slightly before taking the telephone. I only gave my parents a sketch of the whole event. When darkness fell, I was barred in a cell. I spent the day in the cell polishing a confession whose only significance was its power to distract. A few days went by and I hadn't heard from my parents. I sank into deep melancholia. A few days later Himani visited me in the detention center.

"Why are you here?" I asked.

She took off her veil, "I found a witness."

"Witness," I stared at her.

"He has met Bill Singh once," she said.

"What is that to me?" I cut in.

She stood up, signalling to the officer that she had finished with me.

"Could you drop the charge?" I stood up.

"Sit down," a policeman ordered.

"This is a public-prosecuting case," she said.

A sharp pain stabbed at my leg.

"Sit down," the policeman repeated.

I gazed at her distant receding figure. I turned around and gave the policeman an indignant look.

"Sit down," the policeman shouted.

I returned to the cell and wrote out my rage and bewilderment, which gradually became a form of catharsis leading to understanding. The next day Himani came again.

"You look rather pale. What's wrong with you?" she said, but I ignored her. All she could manage was a thin, wan smile.

"I must ask you a favour," she got straight to the point.

"He told me a story," she told me all he said, word for word.

4 CHAPTER SURVIVOR

Bill Singh was born in an ordinary family. He was looking for work. By pure chance he found a rare message he needed in a little employment agency. He packed his bag in haste and said goodbye to his parents. He was away for a short while and soon came back.

A look of bemusement spread across his father's face.

"I forgot to bring a thing," he said running to his room.

"He is forever secretive," his mother stared at him in disbelief.

Bill ran away like an arrow. He was relieved to get back in the bus and hit the road again. Bill touched his rucksack in a subconscious. He cleared a passage for himself through the crammed bus and stood immobile by the window. The bus had windows, but stinks with sweat and dirty socks smell. He put up his hand to screen his eyes from the sun. It was a few moments before his eyes became adjusted to the bright glare of the sun. The bus braked suddenly, throwing him to the floor. He was so scared that he broke out in a cold sweat. Bill eased open the rucksack. He was a bit on edge till he saw it was safe. The bus stopped, and crowds of passengers piled off. He was sweating from the intense heat. Gingerly he opened the rucksack. A kitten was curled on a cushion. His eyes beamed with an expression of gentle affection. He put it on the ground. Bill gave the kitten a little stroke, but it kept on mewing. He lifted up a hand to caress the side of its face. The sudden barking frightened it. The kitten got scared and ran and left him all alone.

"Where are you going?" he shouted.

It was a cat-and-mouse game to him. Already he was sweating as the sun beat down upon him. Running made him puff heavily. It was running on the motor way. A car suddenly darted ahead, squeezing past him with only inches to spare. He came out in cold sweat. Bill stopped to look round, and saw the kitten jump quickly behind a tree. He crossed the road in safety and went round to the off side of the tree. It was curled up in a ball. The action of picking the kitchen up had made his back ache. He squatted down on the ground. Soon he got over. Bill found a piece of rope, made a noose, slipped it about the kitten's neck. After a while, he felt much better and he walked on. He felt a current of cool air. The winds came down with the scents of the grass and wild flowers.

"If we keep on our way for another hour we should reach the coach station," he said to the kitten.

Bill delved into his rucksack and pulled out the cat food. It was not moving, as if someone had bewitched it.

"What's the matter with you?"

"You must be thirsty," he said to himself.

He roped the kitten to a branch. Then, he turned around and left. Bill was back in a trice. In his hand, he carried a bottle of water. Bill unscrewed the cap of his water bottle and gave it a drink.

"It isn't a good method," he said, glancing at the rope.

Bill brought the kitten to a pet shop and bought a cage. He arrived at the station soon. The cage was placed on the roof of the coach. The movement of the coach sent him into sleep. He awoke with a numbed feeling in his left leg.

"What's up?" the coach had been parked on the wayside.

"The luggage got lost," a passenger said.

"What!" he ran out of the coach.

There was only an empty cage on the roof of the coach. He was suddenly baffled for he had never met this situation before, "where is my cat?"

The driver pointed to a jungle. Bill frantically ran for the jungle, but found nothing. The sun was covered by the dark clouds. Thunder rumbled and lightning flashed. The wind howled, trees crashed and rain slashed down. He got soaked to the skin. The road was filled with puddles from the rain. A leaf drifted along with the waves. Soon dark clouds dispersed. The drizzle had now stopped and the sun was breaking through. Bill had to slog up a steep muddy incline. It took a long time to wash the mud out of his shoes. He called his cat by its name. A number of birds were circling overhead. A wounded bird fluttered to the ground. Suddenly a cat sprang at the bird. The cat whirled round at the sound of its name.

"Where have you been?" he picked up his kitten.

The gentlest of his caresses would contort its already tense body. His sense of triumph was short-lived. He had a poor sense of direction and soon got lost. It was a time of confusion, anxiety and despair. Bill tried to follow his own footsteps in the mud and tripped on a rock...

She was so uninteresting that I could hardly keep my eyes open.

"Are you listening to me?" suddenly she asked.

The policeman gave me a push.

"What's up?" I awoke from my sleep and flicked the spittle off the corner of my mouth.

"She's asking you a question," the policeman said to me.

"What did you say?" I asked.

For a long while she remained speechless. There followed an undignified slamming of door. Within a matter of days I was bound over for trial.

"It might as well have been a dream," I thought.

I began to have a sinking feeling that I was not going to get rid of her. "She had no concrete evidence," I comforted myself. Waiting for the result was torture. I awake with the ringing of a telephone bell. I picked up the phone immediately and heard the familiar voice.

"Have you met my daughter yet?" he asked.

"What's up?" I said.

"What did she say to you?" he asked.

"She told me everything," I blurted out.

I realized that I made a big mistake. The silence that followed seemed unnatural. I liked to read the newspaper everyday. One day morning, I learned the sad news about a well-known doctor, who jumped to his death. I had a hunch. I just hope I was wrong. Sleep eluded me. The rest of the morning passed in a blur. I was once more jarred awake by the ringing telephone. I was told that the charges were dropped. I gave a start of astonishment, and stood still.

"Are you listening?"

It was like a dream ended.

"I'm listening," I said quickly.

"The formal document will be delivered within two days," the man continued.

"Thank you," I said.

He hung up when our talk was through. I breathed a sigh of relief. It was not long before the telephone rang again.

"You have an express mail."

"I will arrive shortly," I ran down the stairs like greased lightning.

I received my express mail and was delirious with joy. I stopped by the newsagent's on my way hotel. I just glanced at the headlines. Just then, a bullet streaked across the sky. The gun shot caused uproar in the crowd.

I dropped the newspaper and ran away swiftly. I withdrew to my rented room and took a long slow breath, inhaling deeply. I suddenly found that my leg was bleeding. I looked at myself in the mirror again and again, I found blood was still oozing from the wound.

"There was just a little bleeding. Nothing serious." I said to myself.

I explored the wound with my finger, trying to establish its extent. Just then the phone rang. I was so scared that I broke out in a cold sweat. I tensed my muscles to stop them from shaking. I brought out the SIM card and flushed it down the toilet. I took a deep breath. Trembling, I put the phone down. The telephone rang again almost immediately.

"You can't run away for ever," I looked in the mirror and said.

I stopped at the threshold of the drawing room and crawled under the window. The telephone never stopped ringing. After drawing the curtains, I answered it.

"Hello," I leaned across the desk and lowered my voice.

There were low, muffled voices rising from the receiver. "You have takeout on the reception desk."

"Thank you," I replied as I hung up the telephone.

I stood up and straightened my clothes. I retrieved my takeout from the reception. I raced into the bedroom with my package, excitedly pulling at the wrappings. I chewed a mouthful of popcorn and reached for the remote control and pressed the "red" button. There was nothing except sport and repeats on TV. I turned around and took a can of beer from the fridge. I slaked my thirst with three cans of beer. I recalled every detail of the shooting.

"I fell and grazed my knees," I looked at my wound and said.

"This has happened by sheer accident," I thought.

A lazy somnolence descended on me. I was too tired to keep my eyes open. I lay down on the soft, comfortable bed. The moment I closed my eyes, I fell asleep. I turned over in bed and bumped my arm against on the remote control. I was disturbed and awakened by the TV. I came fully awake to hear the bath running. I sat up and turned off the water. I felt wide awake in bed-I'd drunk too much beer so I tried to read myself to sleep. News on TV caught my attention. I heard all about the shooting on the news. I was satisfied that it was an accident and fell into a deep dreamless sleep. I awoke next morning to brilliant sunshine streaming into my room. I yawned and stretched. The relief was indescribable. A great weight lifted from me. I decided to leave Dehradun. I passed on the news to my grandparents. My grandparents were all agog to see me. I promptly went into the bedroom and started packing. In spite of one or two minor mishaps everything was going swimming. I packed and checked out of the hotel. Having not yet lunched, I went to the refreshment bar for ham sandwiches. A car came from nowhere, and I had to jump back into the hedge just in time. With immense relief I stopped running.

"Mind the car!" a man yelled.

The car hit me on a crossing. I recovered from a faint. When I opened my eyes, I saw a lamp suspended from the ceiling.

"Where am I now?" I asked.

I was shocked to see a woman, wrinkled and black, standing in front of me.

"Mum," I said.

Suddenly I felt a sharp pain in my shoulder.

"The doctor advised you to take a complete rest," my mother said.

"Would you like to tell me what happened?" I held on to my mother's arm.

"A car shot out of a junction and bumped into you," my mother said.

"Police have so far failed to find the culprit."

All the days I was sick my mother had nursed me. My illness had taken a turn for the better. I was already walking normally and doing remedial exercises. Taking a walk everyday was one of my personal laws. I had a sense of deja vu because I could recognise everything in this hospital. Bored out of my mind, I stated out of the window with unseeing eyes. The night was pressing up against the windows. I flopped down upon the bed and rested my tired feet. I went to sleep, and at one o'clock in the morning I woke up. A figure flashed past the window.

"Who are you?" I asked.

The sound of the footsteps died away. I dragged myself wearily out of bed at eight o'clock this morning. I was far too scared to tell anybody. Just then the door opened.

"You look pale and tired," my mother said.

"I didn't sleep well last night," I answered.

"Why?"

"I don't know," I said.

"You are thinking too much," my mother said.

I gave a wry smile. I went for a walk, with the breakfast over. The past few days had seemed comparatively flat and empty. I had become familiar with the hospital. I was bored and desired to go home, but my application was denied. I glued my doctor's cup and saucer together as a practical joke. It was probably just a joke to me, but it wasn't funny to the doctor. I was summoned before the doctor.

"Your sense of humour was really unsettling," said the doctor gravely.

"I'm innocent," I said.

"I wish it were true," he looked at me.

I departed without uttering a word, and then I made an April fool of my roommate. If my roommate gave me half a chance I could make him look stupid. One day he just upped and left. I nailed the chair to the floor. I was waiting for the poor guy to take a pratfall. At this juncture the door opened.

"Your eyes say that you've been upto mischief again," the doctor said.

I closed my eyes.

"Someone had played a trick on patients, stretched a piece of string at the top of those steps." a nurse ran up to him breathing heavily.

"It has got to be stopped. I've had enough of it." said the doctor angrily.

Subsequently, my belongings were taken out of the room and left in the corridor.

"This is a great prank to pull on your roommate," my mother said to me with slight irony.

I had made myself fiercely unpopular in certain circles. I was put in the ICU, and I loved it. Everything seemed so clean and fresh. I made a careful study of the medical instruments in the ICU. I must confess I knew iatrology. Thus, I turned to the patient. I knew for a fact that ICU was very expensive in India. To my surprise, his humble origins. India's post-independence constitution set a goal of eliminating caste-based discrimination, but the caste system still shaped nearly every facet of Indian life. I felt a stirring of curiosity. I suddenly heard a voice behind me.

"What are you doing?" the doctor broke into the room.

"I don't do anything," I answered.

He turned and left the room. I let out my breath in a long sigh. As I went and sat next to him, my attention was suddenly drawn to a notepad. The notepad consisted of vertical and horizontal lines.

"What's this?" I put on my glasses.

I was greeted by a shocking sight. Illiteracy was a major problem in some developing countries. Bit by bit I began to understand what he was trying to say. For the first time I felt that I had achieved something. The story began with a boy. Great men had often risen from poverty, but this rule cannot apply to India. The leaves were inclined to scorch in hot sunshine. The drought had severely disrupted agricultural production. The grass withered because there was no water. The unusually hot sun had fried up the crops. All people's hope rested upon religion. The food was presented to monkeys. Hindus revered them as a symbol of the monkey deity Hanuman, whose simian army helped rescue Sita, the god Rama's wife, from a demon king, according to a Sanskrit epic. People entertained them as honoured guests. Monkeys could not understand human capricious behavior. Monkeys let their eyes settled upon food. At the sight of the monkey catcher, they were too frightened to move. A hungry baby finished up all its mother's breast milk and still expected more. Mother's love was the greatest love in the world. The mother jumped off the tree. Its companions continued to lie on the trees, awaiting developments. The monkey made a long arm for the peach and climbed to a tree and devoured half a peach. They could hardly sit still and itched to have a go. A courageous monkey snatched two apples and ran away. The monkeys knew it would be dangerous to leave the woods, but they were desperate. Faced with a table of goodics they forgot their table manners and ate their heads off. These monkeys cleared out the temple. A contest developed for the food. The major primate problem lied not so much in external invasion as in its internal strife. It was the law of the jungle, the law of nature. The female monkey held its baby in its arm and carried a fat bunch of grapes in one hand. A strong monkey made a snatch at its grapes. They had at each other with fits and feet. Just then, the monkey king hurried across to them and picked up the grapes. The struggle had just come to an end but for the female monkey, the suffering had just begun. Its dazed eyes stared at the ground. It suddenly noticed that its child was lost. It spent a fruitless ten minutes walking up and down the high street, desperately avoiding speeding cars. In people's ears the grieved shouts resound. Never in its life had it felt so alone, so abandoned. For a few seconds it watched the unearthly lights on the water. Suddenly, it sprang up with a howl. It headed straight for a wire pole. Its child crumpled, falling at its feet, sobbing and moaning on the ground. It picked up its crying child. Its child was not breathing. The little monkey accidentally electrocuted itself. The female monkey's ears were sharply attuned to a baby's cry. It could see its child quite distinctly when it rubbed the mists out of its eyes. It walked up to the pram, leaving behind its child's body. It picked up the girl and gave her a grape.

"Hey," the baby's brother shouted.

He picked up a stone hit it to go. The stone hit it on the head. It was rendered unconscious by the blow.

"It dies," it was as if all eyes were focused on him.

"Death and suffering will visit on our village, "the village head's face paled with disappointment; perhaps with anger as well.

"It had a terrible accident, but at all events it wasn't killed." a monk said.

"What should I do?" the young man asked.

"You don't need to do anything," the village head said. "Your family will be evicted."

"Believe me, it's not dead." he said.

"Who can prove it?" the village head asked.

"Veterinarian," he blurted out.

Then, he turned around and left. He held the monkey in his arm and knocked before going in. He wiped the sweat off his face and looked around and seemed surprised to find the big house empty.

"Where is the veterinarian?" he asked.

"The veterinarian went to the town to see his daughter," the veterinarian's neighbor answered.

"Thanks," he went out of the veterinarian's home and came back a few minutes later. He picked out an empty cage and put the monkey in. He made a beeline for the bus station. He was so worried that he looked like a cat on hot bricks. After a half-hour-long wait, the coach finally got to. The cage was placed on the roof of the coach. The coach jolted badly over the rough road. He felt a current of cool air blowing in his face. The sun went in, and the breeze became cold. He yawned, not troubling to cover his mouth. The moment he closed his eyes, he fell asleep. When he woke again he found the coach had arrived at the station. All the passengers got off. He looked up and saw the empty cage.

"Do you see my monkey?" he asked several times, but no one answered. He went back by the same route and frantically ran for the jungle, but found nothing. The sun was covered by the dark clouds. Thunder rumbled and lightning flashed. The wind howled, trees crashed and rain slashed down. He got soaked to the skin. The road was filled with puddles from the rain. Soon dark clouds dispersed. The drizzle had now stopped and the sun was breaking through. He had to slog up a steep muddy incline. It took a long time to wash the mud out of his shoes. He hit upon a strange idea that he wanted to catch a monkey, but he had no experience at it. He was never more clever than when absolutely at his wit's end. He thought of the monkey catcher. He bribed the monkey catcher with costly presents. The monkey catcher put up a trap in a relatively short time. Time passed, and still monkey did not appear. He finally came back empty-handed. He came home to an empty house. His parents had left with his sisters. He asked one or two of his neighbors about it. He found it was no use asking them. They didn't know anything. He accidentally unearthed a crayon picture. In his opinion, that picture was the best of those his sister had drawn. His sister depicted a ship on the picture. This took him back

"They went on vacation to Andaman islands," he thought.

His father promised that within 100 days they would go to that place. The scheme seemed a bit airy fairy to him. He had concluded that he had no choice but to accept his father's words as the truth. After several setbacks, he reached the port at last. He didn't have enough money. He could only buy the cheapest ticket. It was the first time he had been on a ship, and he had a very uncomfortable time of it, throwing up like a sick cat. And the light was shining, slow and feeble. God and men had completely forgotten him. The little room was windowless and oppressive. Everything grew more and more duller, and he no longer knew how time passed. The novelty of his surroundings soon wore off. He lay back and closed his eyes. All of a sudden there was a terrific bang. He didn't know what was going on. He sat up in alarm and was scared out of his wit and walked on trembling with fear. It was pitch-dark in the corridor and he couldn't see a thing. He found the elevator was out of service due to a blackout. The air conditioning had broken down. The cargo hold had awful stink. The emergency lights became the only illuminant. He was shocked by what he saw. The interior of the cargo hold showed a variety of cages. The cages smelled of excrement. He concluded that these animals belonged to a circus. Just then, a hamster got through the wire at the front of its cage. The hamster had hardly come out when he caught it. It initially had no fear of man. He gently stroked its face. Suddenly, he felt his hand bitten. He snatched his hand away with a cry of pain. It slipped off when it saw what was going to happen. In a moment it had disappeared amid of the gloom of the floor. He was plainly annoyed and vented his anger on monkeys. A monkey held out its hand and grasped his collar. He felt short of breath. The cage was a couple of hand-spans from his face. A crowbar stood in one corner of the cage. He picked up it in an emergency. Its grip slackened on his collar. He took a deep breath and made a face and stuck out his tongue at the monkey. Just then, he saw a light at the far end.

"What are you doing here?"

He did not know what to reply.

"A rush-repair is being done on the line and the power supply will return to normal in half an hour," a security guard said.

The cargo hold suddenly lit up.

"Oh, great!" the security guard turned off his flashlight.

The security guard looked up and found he had vanished. He got into the elevator and sailed to the top floor. The door opened and he stood there stupefied by almost could not believe his own eyes. In the hall there was a long table spread with food. The smell from the food made his mouth water. He swallowed hard and left the elevator. Food was included in the ticket. He greedily shovelled the food into his mouth. He paused, patted his breast, and belched. He was so thirsty that he drank a liter of tomato juice. He took a big gulp and chocked and splashed tomato juice over his coat. He wiped his coat with a tissue. Ten minutes later he re-entered his room. A sudden dizziness overpowered him. Because he was seasick, he brought up his lunch. He felt a tremendous pressure on his chest. He couldn't get back to sleep. He was listless and pale and wouldn't eat much. He felt cut off from the outside world. He started to sit up, grimaced, and sank back weakly against the pillow. Now and then he heard the engines revving. He decided first to go out on the deck for a breath of open air. A relative calm reigned over the ship. Gasping for breath, he leaned against the door. This eerie calm was an illusion. Some guests relined in lounge chairs. The sea was blue, and white puffy clouds sailed by. The high wind passed and the sea was calm again. A mariner was surprised to find the seawater flowing backward. The mariner felt it his duty to report it to the captain. The captain guessed it was nothing serious. He was doing nothing to intervene in the crisis. The animals were cognizant of the problem. They totally lost control.

"What do you want to do?" the boy shouted.

The animals were very disobedient towards him.

"Who can help me?" looking round, he realized with a shock that he was the only passenger left in the cargo hold.

The elephants trumpeted and stamped their feet at his approach. It all happened so suddenly that he didn't know what to do. He moved backwards till he was pressed against the wall. Then he noticed the ship was bouncing up and down as if someone were jumping on it. He climbed the rickety stairway. There was not a single soul in the rooms of the ship. Passengers escaped from the ship's exits by sliding down emergency chutes. He saw them through the window pane. He could find no way out in the face of difficulties. Presently a lifeboat in sight, and his face lighted; he gazed a moment, and then turned sorrowfully away. It was kaput. The earthquake caused tsunami, which devastated coastal regions. Huge waves surged over the lifeboats. In a twinkling, they dipped below the surface of the water. He saw a huge wave coming quickly toward him. Suddenly he thought of animals. He ran to the cargo hold and picked up the crowbar and forced the lock of the monkeys' cage. He skirted round the edge of the room to the elephants' cage. His effort helped the elephants gain their freedom. The elephants became good helpers of him. A door was kicked open with a bang. The horses were saved safely. They were in a race against time. He mopped perspiration from his forehead. He took a deep breath, and began to climb the stairs. He stopped to look round, and saw a lion jump quickly behind an artificial tree. His hesitation was only momentary. He walked quickly to the cage. The lion was motionless, like a curled up, oblivious kitten. He was moved with compassion. Just then, a huge wave washed over the deck of the ship. The monkeys were swept out to sea. The impact blew out some of the windows and the sea came rushing in. He could smell the salty tang of the sea. He managed to prise off the lock with the crowbar. The hungry lion reverted to its nature. It made at him. He ducked in time to save his head from a blow from the lion. He unconsciously moved back a pace or two. The lion roared once, and sprang. He swung the crowbar at its head with all his might. The deflection of the crowbar by the tree. He was full of remorse. Just then, the lion flung itself at him with bared fangs and slashed a rent in his coat. His wound burned like fire. At the same moment the lion was closing in upon him. He thought it scented blood. The lion swooped down upon him. At the crucial moment, an elephant gave it a swift kick in the behind. The lion lost its balance, staggered front against the rail and toppled over. The sea frothed over his feet.

"The ship is sinking," he came out in cold sweat.

He climbed the steps and proceeded along the upstairs hallway. He strode to the elevator and punched the button. He took the elevator to the ground floor. He burst out as the door was flung open. A powerful current spurted out. The ship was now leaning at a 30 degree angle. The sea cast up him on the deck. He got a purchase on the rail. Huge waves surged over the ship. Somebody punched him in the stomach hard and he let go of the handle, the air in his lungs, and his dinner all at once.

"Who are you?" he looked up to see the lion.

Its tail cocked up. He thought it'd stop pestering him, but it only seemed to make him worse. The lion pounced upon him. As he sidestepped, it hit him on the left hip. Swashing against the ship, the breakers sent up a fountain of spray. They were swept away by the strong current. The ship instantly tilted, filled and sank. The noise nearly frightened him out of sense. A relative calm reigned over the sea. Suddenly, a corpse floated across the sea. He grabbed the corpse's life jacket. He was trying to find his way out when he suddenly heard some noise above him. A monkey made a persistent effort to search for its companions lost in the tsunami. All these things gave him hope. He made for the lifeboat and hung on for dear life. The monkey snarled at the intruder. He felt as if all his strength had gone. Its paws lacerated his arm. His resistance suddenly stiffened because there was no room for retreat. The monkey retreated. He climbed the rickety lifeboat. He stretched out on the boat and kicked off his shoes. The monkey crept to the edge of the lifeboat. He stole a glance at the monkey and discovered that it was a female monkey. He allowed himself a wry smile. Suddenly, his stomach growled. He sighed, turning away and surveying the sea. A life jacket floated in the sea. He reached out a hand towards the life jacket and changed his coat for it. Since then, more goods had been discovered. He fished up a pair of sunglasses and a tin of beef. He was delirious with joy. He put the glasses on and opened the tin. The monkey pounced upon him. He slipped and fell heavily. The tin fell into the sea. He glowered and glared, but it steadfastly refused to look his way. An idea came across his mind. For a few minutes, he was allowed to rest on the floor and looked dazed, if not comfortable. The monkey tried not to take any notice at first but then it was cheated. He grabbed its arm. He shook it off. The monkey fell down to the sea. It struggled wildly, going under and resurfacing at regular intervals. He caught himself feeling almost sorry for poor monkey. Then he extended his hand. Just then, the lion made at him...

Suddenly, a hand touched my shoulder. I was so nervous that my palms were all cold and sweating. I awoke next morning to brilliant sunshine streaming into my room. I needed space to think everything over and began to keep a diary. There was so little to go on, I can only surmise what happened. I read through pages and pages of the notepad. I found two pages had been torn out of the notepad. I didn't know what was going on. I stared detachedly into the middle distance, towards nothing in particular. My roommate had lapsed into unconsciousness again. The sky was dimmed by clouds. The clouds were so dense that it seemed as if the sun were setting early. There was only one sliver of light in the darkness. There seemed to be something fishy going on. Half a minute later a shot rang out. I felt a sharp pain and looked down to see blood pouring from my arm. Luckily I was not very seriously wounded. After about 30 minutes the police arrived. The crowds gathered about the scene of the crime. I was taken from the ICU. After the doctor treated the wound, my arm was carefully bandaged. I was then taken by police car to the police station. The police completed a preliminary survey after asking dozens of detailed questions. After a few days I received the final report. I turned to the very end of the report, to read the final words. They came to conclusions diametrically opposed to mine. They thought it was an accident. This question placed me in a quandary. The only change was that the worker replaced the broken pane of glass. I vacated the ICU and went to live in the common ward. Peace was finally restored in the hospital. It wasn't the peaceful, composed experience I had expected. Within a matter of days I was heartbroken at the news of his death. I made the mistake of trying to extract further information from nurse. His name was expunged from the record books. When I tried to enter the ICU, the guard at the door challenged me. I refrained from further speech, and descended to the ground floor again. Suddenly, I realized I'd left my bag at the ICU. Eventually I turned around and went back to that room. There was not in the ICU a chair or a desk I didn't know. My nose twitched and I began to weep.

"What are you doing?" a nurse asked.

"I left my bag somewhere near here," I then turned around, walked away. The sun caught the panes and flashed back at me. I stared out at the impeccably manicured garden. I turned to look back, but by then the nurse was out of sight. I noticed that the room number.

"321," the truth at last dawned on me.

Just then, I saw a nurse coming towards me from a long way off. "The doctor allows you to leave the hospital."

I turned away, and set off towards my room. I yanked open the drawer and took out my cell phone and automatically without any thought, dialled the number. "I want to see you."

"Please do not leave the hospital before being formally discharged," the nurse cut in.

"You can go out," I said in a bored tone.

I moved away from the hospital. As I had expected, she was tardy in her response. I didn't have incontrovertible evidence of what took place.

"Some solid evidence is what is required," I sucked in a deep lungful of air.

Suddenly, my cell phone rang and I picked up the cell phone.

"Where are you now?" the voice at the other end of the line was serious.

I gave a wry smile, "you don't know? Your daughter knew."

"I want to see you," he continued.

"No problem," I blurted out.

After hung up, I let out a long sigh, mainly of relief, partly of nervousness. I immediately regretted having said these. Things done can not be undone.

For a few minutes I sat on the sofa watching the clock. The hands of the clock on the wall moved with a slight click. As each minute passed, I became increasingly anxious. Suddenly there came a rat-a-tat on the door and when I opened it I locked myself in.

Presently he heard the sound of my ragged breathing, "do you need help?"

"No," I mopped perspiration from my forehead.

At last the door opened and a fatherly-looking man appeared.

"Nice to meet you," he extended his hand and glanced at me with a pleased smile.

"I have the impression that we have met once before," I said.

He simply denied that such a thing had ever happened.

"Oh, I made a mistake." I broke the silence.

He made a faint attempt at a laugh.

"Can I sit down now?" he asked suddenly.

"Of course," I said.

I looked him up and down.

"What are you looking at?" he asked.

"You don't look like a bad man," I answered.

He permitted himself a small mirthless smile, "how much does my daughter know about this matter?"

"You aren't a businessman, are you? Let's make a trade." I said.

"Trade!" he looked at me.

"Are you telling me the whole truth?" I asked.

He burst into uncontrollable laughter at I'd said.

"No problem," he replied.

"Once upon a time," he continued.

I interjected, "you must tell the truth."

"I see," he smiled and said.

In all fairness I had to admit that he had a talent for recollection and anecdote. The story opened with a robbery. A teenager was caught trying to rob a store with a banana - then ate the makeshift weapon to destroy the evidence. The teenager pretended ignorance about the accident. The store manager toyed with the idea of calling the police, but in the end he didn't. The teenager walked out of the bank with a self-confident swagger. The amusing news travelled fast. The store was besieged with visitors. Children mimicked the teenager's voice and gestures perfectly. The visitors drove the salesclerks crazy. An old man sat down and put on a pair of glasses.

"What can I do for you?" a salesclerk asked.

"What?" the old man asked.

"What can I do for you?" the salesclerk repeated.

"What?" the old man said.

"What can I do for you?" the salesclerk said aloud.

The old man hauled himself to his feet and slammed the counter with the flat of his hand. He opened his mouth and his dentures dropped off. The salesclerk was incensed. He was in a bit of flap and pressed the manual fire alarm button by mistake. The siren filled the air.

"What's wrong?" the store manager asked.

It all happened so quick that the salesclerk could do nothing.

"Spit it out! Have you lost your tongue?" the store manager said.

"Robbery," the salesclerk said, without thinking.

"Who is the robber?" the store manager shouted.

The salesclerk took a quick glance around and then pointed to a young man.

"Catch him," the store manager ordered.

"I don't have a banana," the young man explained.

Then the young man heard footsteps: someone sprinting towards him from behind. The young man turned tail and fled in the direction of the main road. The salesclerk felt a tug on his shirt sleeve.

"I'm quite deaf- you'll have to speak up." the old man said.

The salesclerk took a look at the old man and said, "Don't forget your dentures."

The young man migrated to Dehradun in search of work. He was quite unconscious of his appearance now. Just then, a police car zoomed by very close to him. The young man broke out in a cold sweat and bent his head instinctively to avoid being recognized. It dawned on him that he was lost. The first time he came to Dehradun was ten years ago. He thought he knew this area but this street wasn't ringing any bells for him. It bewildered and depressed him. The sound of drums, from a great distance, growing louder. He stopped his pace and spotted a truck. The truck carried three cages. The animals were kept under inhumane conditions. A bear was very still, its eyes glassy. A tiger paced up and down in its cage.

"Mum, a circus is in town now." a boy said to his mother.

It was all a publicity stunt. He didn't have any interest in animal performances. The young man needed a guide urgently. He stopped to ask the way. The truck driver helped him. He got into the passenger seat. The young man stared unseeing out of the window. The truck driver braked suddenly to avoid a cat. They went on, and after a while the truck was going to cross the road. Suddenly, they heard a strange sound which made them frightened.

"What's wrong?" the young man stared at the driver in consternation.

"It's nothing serious," the driver gave a little cough.

The young man felt the atmosphere grow tense.

"How far is it to the hotel?" the young man asked.

The driver evaded his eyes and fell into silence.

"Stop, I want to get off." the young man said.

The driver stopped the car and dodged into the grove. The young man gave a wry smile. In the same instant he flung open the car door. A lion bounded on him. The young man slipped into the car and closed the door.

"Where does it come from?" he cast his mind back to the cages. One of the cages was wrapped in black cloth.

"Who opened the cage door?" he thought.

There was the sound of breaking glass, and a paw reached in through the driver's side window. Luckily, the lion stuck its paw in the window. The young man took a deep breath. Suddenly, the lion pulled open the car door. He panicked, and his first thought was that it would kill him, so he struggled and screamed. He whooped until he was hoarse, but it was of no use. The lion made at him, but he dodged it. He wrenched open the passenger door and leapt from the truck. The lion jerked its wrist free. Blood was pouring from its wound. In a moment he was gone.

The young man concealed himself under the truck, but that didn't mean he could rest easy. The lion picked up his scent. It crawled under the truck. He crawled on his hands and knees out onto the truck. The lion stood up and indignation blazed in its eyes. It came closer to the young man and raised its paw. He stood on the roof of the truck. Abruptly the lion halted its attack and turned and walked away. Its conduct was a mystery to him. It dived into the grove and disappeared. An awful scream singed the sky. The lion was back in a trice. Death frightened him, specifically his own death. He looked at it with a mixture of horror and awe. The lion ate a great big dinner. He was really terrified to witness the slaughter. In the face of dangers, it was better for one to take positive. He leaped on to the cage with a thump. The noise aroused the sleeping bear. The bear continued to paw and claw frantically at the chain mesh. Its paws lacerated his feet. He jumped in the driver side and started the truck, the tyres screaming as his foot jammed against the accelerator. The lion flung itself to the truck. He drove faster, watching the needle flick up to a hundred km. It crawled along the roof of the truck until it reached the windscreen. The lion tried to cling to the edge by its paws. The young man gasped, staring through the windscreen, and a tail as thick as a python smash into it. The windscreen wipers clacked back and forth. This was an ineffective method of controlling the lion. He spun the wheel sharply and made a U turn in the middle of the road. The crisis here caught the police attention. A fleet of police cars suddenly arrived. Dozens of officers piled out. A policeman fired a warning shot. The young man slowed the truck and began driving up a narrow road. The lion put its paw into the cab. It found the young man's cheeks and raked them with its nails. Blood ran from his forehead into his eyes, blurring his vision. The truck veered out of control, overturned and smashed into a wall.

"Is this the end of the story?" I asked.

Himani's father nodded his head.

"How many cops are involved in this?" I asked.

"17," he answered.

"Who opened the cage door?" I asked.

"I don't know."

"The cage was unlocked when the young man arrived," I affirmed.

He began to giggle.

"What are you laughing at?" I looked at him.

"You know too much," he took out a gun.

"What do you want to do?" I shouted.

He roared with laughter, shaking in his chair. I pounced on the man.

"You're flying in the face of the law," I said.

"So what?" he punched me on the nose.

I snatched the gun from his hand. Suddenly the door was opened and Himani entered.

"What are you doing?" she stared at us, thunderstruck.

He and I were struggling for the gun when it went off! The bullet punctured her heart. She fell dead immediately. The death of his daughter had hit him hard. He picked up his daughter and hugged her tight. Tears streamed down his face.

I didn't know how to treat myself as an observer. Human nature was complicated. In order to survive, we had to be independent, strong and tough. We left ourselves wide open to accusations of double standards and hypocrisy. As my mind drifted off my cell phone rang.

"Who?" he asked.

"My father," I answered.

"My father will come in a moment," I added.

"You are the senator's son," he said.

I threw him a faint smile. It was plain to me that he was having a nervous, breakdown. I couldn't help feeling sorry for the poor man. The silence was broken by a sudden knock at the door. He shut his eyes involuntarily when he pulled the trigger. I was stultified, shocked. The door was kicked open with a bang and cops charged in.

"Who is survivor?" I asked.

The end